# Little Women

Retold from the Louisa May Alcott
original by Deanna McFadden

*Illustrated by Lucy Corvino*

**STERLING CHILDREN'S BOOKS**
New York

# STERLING CHILDREN'S BOOKS
New York

An Imprint of Sterling Publishing
387 Park Avenue South
New York, NY 10016

STERLING CHILDREN'S BOOKS and the distinctive Sterling Children's Books logo are
trademarks of Sterling Publishing Co., Inc.

ISBN 978-1-4027-1236-4

**Library of Congress Cataloging-in-Publication Data**
McFadden, Deanna.
 Little women / abridged by Deanna McFadden; illustrated by Lucy Corvino; retold from the
Louisa May Alcott original.
  p. cm.—(Classic starts)
 Summary: An abridged version of the novel chronicling the joys and sorrows of the four March
sisters as they grow into young women in mid-nineteenth-century New England.
  ISBN 1-4027-1236-7
 [1. Sisters—Fiction. 2. Family life—New England—Fiction. 3. New England—History—19th cen-
tury—Fiction.] I. Corvino, Lucy, ill. II. Alcott, Louisa May, 1832–1888. Little women. III. Title. IV.
Series.
PZ7.M4784548Li 2004
[Fic]—dc22

                                                                        2004013668

Distributed in Canada by Sterling Publishing
c/o Canadian Manda Group, 165 Dufferin Street
Toronto, Ontario, Canada M6K 3H6
Distributed in the United Kingdom by GMC Distribution Services,
Castle Place, 166 High Street, Lewes, East Sussex, England BN7 1XU
Distributed in Australia by Capricorn Link (Australia) Pty. Ltd.
P.O. Box 704, Windsor, NSW 2756, Australia

For information about custom editions, special sales, and premium and corporate purchases,
please contact Sterling Special Sales at 800-805-5489 or specialsales@sterlingpublishing.com.

Printed in China
Lot#:
26 28 30 29 27 25
12/18

www.sterlingpublishing.com/kids

# CONTENTS

# CHAPTER 1

## Playing Pilgrims

ᘯ

While the snow fell quietly outside their New England home, the four March sisters stayed warm by the fire in their cozy living room.

"Christmas won't be the same without presents," grumbled fifteen-year-old Jo, lying on the rug.

Her older sister Meg sighed as she looked at her old dress. "It's not much fun being poor."

"It's not fair that some girls have lots of pretty things, and other girls don't have any at all," sniffed Amy, who at twelve was the youngest.

"But we've got a mother and a father who love us very much, and we've always got each other," thirteen-year-old Beth said happily from her corner. Her words seemed to cheer up the others.

"Father's been gone for a long time, and we don't know when he'll be coming back," said Jo.

Meg insisted, "This is going to be a hard winter for everyone. We shouldn't be buying presents while so many men are suffering during the war. We should make sacrifices!" But even as she said these kind words, Meg still longed for pretty things at Christmas.

Jo said, "We've only got a dollar each and that's not going to help the army much." She was the bookworm in the family and wanted to buy a new novel. Beth longed for music, and Amy dreamed of coloring pencils to help her draw.

Jo continued, "Mother wouldn't mind if we spent our dollars on ourselves and had a little fun. We work hard."

The chimes announced that it was six o'clock. Beth put a pair of her mother's slippers near the fire to warm. Jo noticed how old and worn they were. She said, "We should get Marmee a new pair!"

When Beth said *she* was going to buy the slippers with her dollar, Jo insisted *she* should be the one to buy them because their father had told her to take special care of their mother while he was away. Meg thought that *she* should since she was the oldest.

Beth said, "I've got an idea! Let's all buy something for Marmee, and not for ourselves."

All the girls thought this was a wonderful idea. Meg said she would buy Marmee some gloves.

Jo exclaimed, "Satin slippers! The best I can get."

Beth chimed in, "Lovely hemmed handkerchiefs."

Amy thought for a minute as she pulled one of her blond curls. "I'll get Marmee a little bottle of perfume. This way I'll still have something for myself."

Jo was excited. "I can't wait to surprise her!" She turned to her sisters. "We'll go shopping tomorrow. And remember, we've got to rehearse our Christmas play." Jo started marching around the living room. In a few minutes, the girls were laughing so hard they almost didn't hear their mother come in from the cold.

"Glad to see you girls are having so much fun," Marmee said. "Did you all have a good day?"

As Marmee took off her wet clothes, put on her warm slippers, and sat down in front of the fire, the girls flew into action. Jo stoked the fire, Meg got dinner ready, Beth helped Meg, and Amy told everyone what to do and how to do it.

When all five of them were sitting down at the

dining-room table, Marmee said, "I've got a treat for you girls after supper."

The smiles quickly spread. Jo threw her napkin in the air, crying, "It's a letter. Three cheers for Father!"

Marmee nodded. "Yes, it's a letter from your father. He's well and thinks the winter won't actually be that bad. He sends his love for Christmas, and a special message that I'll save until after dinner."

The girls hurried their meal. They couldn't wait to hear the letter. They missed their father terribly.

After dinner, the four girls cuddled with their mother near the fire. Marmee read, "Tell my girls I think of them all the time. Even though it'll be a long while before I see them, I know they'll act properly and not waste their days being silly. I know when I come home, I'll be prouder than ever of my little women."

The letter convinced the girls to be good while their father was away. Everyone was cheerful as they set about their evening sewing after Hannah had cleared away the plates. Mrs. March reminded the girls how they used to act out scenes from *Pilgrim's Progress*. The girls recalled running through the house with bags on their backs and escaping evil forces.

When it came time for bed, the girls sang, with Beth happily playing the piano. Each performed in her own way: Meg sounded like a flute, Amy chirped like a cricket, and Jo came in when she felt like it—bad timing and all. They had sung before bed since they were small, and even now they were never too old for familiar lullabies.

# CHAPTER 2

# A Merry Christmas

ᘓ

On Christmas morning, each of the four girls woke up to find a copy of *Pilgrim's Progress* under her pillow. Meg told her sisters that she was going to read a little each morning, both to keep her spirits up and to help her be good. Then Jo spoke up.

"Look how good Meg is. Come on, girls, let's do the same."

Soon, all four sisters were seated at the little tables in their bedrooms reading their books. After a half hour, they went downstairs to wish their mother "Merry Christmas," only to find that she wasn't there.

Meg asked where she had gone, and Hannah replied, "Someone came a callin' and your ma went straightaway to see if she could help."

The girls got everything ready to surprise their mother. Jo softened the new slippers by dancing around the room as Meg readied the gift basket. Beth showed off the handkerchiefs, which she had lovingly embroidered with the word "Mother."

"Where's Amy's perfume?" Meg asked.

Jo replied, "She went to find a piece of ribbon to tie around the bottle."

A door slammed and the girls heard steps in the hallway.

"Quick," said Jo, "there's Mother. Hide the basket!"

It was only Amy, who looked liked she was up to something.

Meg asked, "What's that behind your back?"

"Now don't laugh at me," Amy said, "but I've exchanged my little bottle for a big one, and I've used up all my money." She took the new beautiful bottle out of the bag to show her sisters, who hugged her. "I was ashamed of my present after reading about being good and kind this morning, so I went to get Marmee something better."

The door banged a second time. Meg shoved the basket under the sofa, and the girls went to the table, eager for their Christmas breakfast. When their mother came into the room, they all cried out, "Thank you for the presents, Marmee. We've already read some, and will read more each day!"

"Merry Christmas, little daughters! I'm glad you're enjoying the books. Now, I want to say something. A very poor family lives nearby. They have no fire and are very hungry. Will you girls give them your breakfast as a Christmas present?"

The girls were desperately hungry after waiting an hour for Marmee, so at first no one said anything. Then, Jo piped up: "I'm so glad we hadn't started yet!"

Beth said she would love to help carry the food to the poor family. And Amy said she would take the cream and the muffins—the food she loved most. Meg was already covering the pancakes and putting the bread on a big plate.

Mrs. March smiled at her daughters. "When we get back, we'll have bread and milk for breakfast. Then, we'll have a wonderful dinner to make up for everything."

They were soon ready and left in the cold to help the family in need. When they arrived, they were shocked to see the bare, unheated, miserable room. A sick mother held her crying baby. Six other children huddled under one blanket, but they managed a smile as the March family came inside.

"Angels have come to help us!" Mrs. Hummel, the mother, cried.

Jo grinned. "Funny angels in hoods and mittens." Everyone laughed.

In a few minutes, the room completely changed. Hannah made a fire with wood she had carried. Mrs. March gave Mrs. Hummel tea and oatmeal. Tenderly, she wrapped the newborn. The four March sisters fed the children near the fire. They were very happy to see their joyful faces.

Once back at home, the girls set out their presents while

their mother was out collecting clothes for the poor Hummels. Jo screamed with glee, "She's coming! Beth, play a tune. Amy, get the door. Three cheers for Marmee!" Jo marched around on her long legs.

Meg brought their smiling mother to her chair. She was touched by her daughters' generosity and happily opened her presents. She tried on the slippers, doused herself with the perfume, put a new handkerchief in her pocket, and said the gloves were a perfect fit. After lots of hugs and kisses, it was time to prepare for that night's play.

A dozen girls from the neighborhood came to watch Jo's love story. All four sisters performed in five thrilling acts, wearing different costumes and remembering all their lines. One of the props fell with a clatter on the unsuspecting audience. Hannah appeared just after the final act to find everyone in a fit of laughter.

She announced, "Time for supper, girls!"

What a surprise! On the table were two different kinds of ice cream, lots of candy, fruit, cake—and four bouquets of flowers! At first, no one spoke. Finally, Beth whispered, "It must be from Santa Claus."

Amy asked, "Is it fairies?"

Meg said, "It must have been Mother."

"Aunt March must have sent it," cried Jo.

"No, you're all wrong," Marmee said. "Old Mr. Laurence sent it."

"The Laurence boy's grandfather?" Meg questioned. "But we don't even know him. What made him send over all this food?"

Marmee replied, "Hannah told one of his servants what you girls did today, so Mr. Laurence wanted to honor you with a special treat. Now, you'll have a little feast to make up for your bread-and-milk breakfast."

Jo said thoughtfully, "His grandson must have given him the idea. I'll bet he's a fine boy."

The girls dug into their delicious treats as they talked about the young man next door and his protective grandfather.

Jo said, "He once brought back my cat, and was very nice about it. I'd like to get to know him. I think he needs some fun."

Marmee agreed. "His manners were very good, and he looks like a nice young gentleman. I should have asked him to come and see your play."

"It's probably a good idea you didn't," laughed Jo. "Just look at us!" She stomped around in her old leather boots for effect.

Meg admired the flowers. Beth hugged her mother and said, "I wish we could send my bunch to Father. I'll bet he isn't having such a merry Christmas."

# CHAPTER 3

# The Laurence Boy

⁓

As Jo read, tears streamed down her slim cheeks. With her pet rat Scrabble nearby, she sat on an old couch in the attic. It was her favorite place in the house; she often went there to eat apples and lose herself in a book. Hearing Meg's call, she yelled, "I'm up here!"

Meg was very excited because they had been invited to a New Year's Eve dance at Sallie Gardiner's house.

"Oh Jo! Marmee said we could go," she cried. "What should we wear?"

"You know we'll wear our old poplin dresses. That's all we have."

"If I only had a silk dress!" Meg sighed. "Mother says I have to wait until I'm eighteen— two whole years away."

"Our poplin dresses are fine. Yours looks just like new. But mine has that burn and tear. What am I going to do?"

Her sister advised, "You'll sit as much as you can with your back to the wall so no one will see the burn."

"And what about my gloves? I spilled lemonade on them and they're ruined, too," Jo thought about the cost for new ones, and said, "I just won't wear any."

"You *must* have gloves, or I won't go," cried Meg. She always wanted to be proper.

They decided each would wear one of Meg's good gloves, and hold one of Jo's spoiled ones. Meg made Jo promise to behave like a lady, and never say things like "Christopher Columbus!" Jo agreed and sent an acceptance to the invitation as soon as she finished her book.

On New Year's Eve, the two older March girls spent a long time getting ready for the party. After one mishap (Jo burned Meg's hair while trying to curl it), both girls were happy with the results. They looked smart and pretty, even if Meg's high-heeled shoes were too tight and Jo's hairpins stuck straight into her scalp. Their mother told them to have a good time.

The girls arrived at Sallie's house and spent a few minutes inspecting themselves in Mrs. Gardiner's dressing-room mirror. Meg worried about her burned hair, and Jo worried about doing something wrong. They developed a system: Meg would lift her eyebrows if Jo acted improperly.

Once downstairs, Meg found a group of girls her age to talk to and was soon dancing, even though her new shoes hurt her feet. Jo desperately wanted to join a group of boys who were talking about skating, which she loved, but Meg's eyebrows went right up—so none of that! Jo tried not to feel so alone and out of place, but when a big redheaded boy came toward her, she disappeared into a curtained closet. Only she wasn't alone: she was face to face with the Laurence boy!

"I'm sorry," Jo blurted out. "I didn't realize anyone was here." She started to back out of the closet when he laughed and said, "Don't mind me. Stay if you like."

"Wouldn't I bother you?"

"Not at all. I came here because I don't know many people and felt a little strange by myself."

"So did I."

Their conversation started awkwardly, for they were both shy. Then Jo thanked him for the Christmas dinner, and he explained it was his grandfather's idea.

"How is your cat, Miss March?"

"Very well, thank you, Mr. Laurence; but my name is just Jo, not Miss March."

He smiled and replied, "Well then, I'm Laurie, not Mr. Laurence."

"Laurie Laurence, what a funny name."

"My name is Theodore, but I don't like it because the boys called me Dora. I made them say Laurie instead."

"And I wish everyone would call me Jo instead of Josephine."

Soon, the two talked like old friends. Jo was excited to learn Laurie had been to school in France. He said that he wasn't that interested in going to college, and Jo said she'd love to live in Italy. They even managed to dance down a long hallway so that Jo could keep her burned dress hidden. They had a wonderful time until Meg called Jo into a side room. Meg sat on a couch holding her foot and looking pale.

"The heel turned and I sprained my ankle." Meg winced. "I don't know how I'll get home."

Jo suggested they get a carriage, but Meg said it would cost too much. They decided Meg should rest until Hannah came to get them, and then she'd try to walk home. Meg sent Jo to bring her coffee.

When Meg took a sip, she spilled coffee all over her dress and ruined her one good glove by trying to wipe away the stains. Laurie appeared with a cup of coffee and offered it to Meg. The three of them had so much fun laughing, playing games, and eating candy that they barely noticed Hannah's arrival. Meg got up too quickly and tried to hide her pain. But when Hannah scolded her, Meg cried.

Jo decided to look for a carriage. She ran into Laurie, who was about to go home. He suggested that they all go home in his grandfather's elegant carriage. What a lovely ride it was! Meg and Jo felt like fancy ladies, and had no trouble passing the time recalling the evening's adventures.

They were just through the front door when both Amy and Beth cried, "Tell us about the party!"

And as Jo wrapped Meg's ankle, the younger girls heard about the burned hair, ruined glove, stained dress, tight shoes, sprained ankle, and all!

# CHAPTER 4

# Burdens

⎯⌒⎯

Now that the holidays were over, the day began sourly. Meg tried to hide her envy of girls who didn't have so many burdens. Jo didn't feel like going back to work. Beth had a headache, and Amy complained because she hadn't finished her schoolwork.

With their hot turnovers in hand, the girls headed outdoors. Marmee smiled and nodded to them from the window. That seemed to brighten their spirits. Meg took being poor the hardest. She loved fine things and had warm memories of better days.

The two older girls had begged to help financially. So Meg worked as a governess for the Kings, and Jo was a companion to their father's elder sister, Aunt March, who was rich and frail. Despite their differences, Jo and Aunt March got along very well. Jo often spent time in the large library when her aunt didn't need her.

The poverty of the family affected the girls differently. While they tried to be cheerful, Beth wept a little because she couldn't afford music lessons. Quiet and shy, she did her lessons at home and spent a lot of time with her dolls. She was a giving child, whose greatest joy was caring for others.

Amy's worst problem was her nose. She blamed Jo, who accidentally dropped her as a baby. All the pinching in the world couldn't give her an aristocratic point. In terms of talent, Amy was the artist, forever drawing flowers, fairies, and all the pretty noses she so desired.

All in all, they were happy girls who found comfort in one another, when the outside world was so disappointing. A hard day's work was rewarded by long conversations after supper when mother and daughters talked for hours.

On this night, Mrs. March told a moving story. While she was cutting jackets, an old man came into the shop. All four of his sons were in the army. Two were killed, one was a prisoner, and the last was sick in a Washington hospital. Marmee said she was grateful to run into a man so accepting of his duty, which made her very thankful for her blessings.

"Tell us another story with a moral," Jo asked. So Marmee began a tale about four girls who had enough to eat, drink, and wear. They had many wonderful friends and a family who loved them very much. Still, these girls weren't happy, always asking for this and wishing for that. All four sisters stole silent glances at one another and sewed faster as their mother continued.

"When you feel unhappy, count your blessings and be grateful—for there are always those in the world with less," Marmee said.

The girls enjoyed the story and all agreed to stop complaining and to find happiness in their own small blessings, keeping Marmee's words very close to their hearts.

# CHAPTER 5

# Being Neighborly

The winter day had brought a great snowfall. As Meg read by the fire with a book, Jo took a broom and shovel outside to clear the walkways in case Beth wanted to get some fresh air. With too much energy to sit by the fire, Jo loved to be outdoors getting exercise, no matter what the weather. In fact, today she had decided to find out more about the lonely Laurence boy.

Jo loved to do daring things, so she threw a snowball at Laurie's window. He opened the window and smiled down at Jo, who waved her broom, yelling, "Hello! Are you sick?"

In a raspy voice, Laurie answered, "I've had a bad cold and have been inside all week."

"What have you been doing to keep busy?"

"Nothing much."

Laurie hadn't been allowed to read. When Jo suggested that his friends should come to visit, Laurie said that boys were too noisy.

"What about a girl then? Someone to play nurse and read to you?"

"Don't know any."

"You know me," Jo laughed.

What a great idea! Jo went back into her house to ask her mother's permission, while Laurie straightened his room and brushed his hair. When Jo appeared on his doorstep, she brought lots of goodies. Meg made a cake, Amy gathered flowers, and Beth sent her three kittens. The gifts were just the right things to help Laurie relax. Jo sat in a big chair and Laurie lay on the sofa. She asked if she could read a book to him, but Laurie said he'd rather talk.

And they did. They talked about Jo's family, and Laurie admitted that he enjoyed looking into their house from his window. Laurie described his tutor, Mr. Brooke. Then, he talked about his grandfather. Jo explained that she didn't go to school and worked for her Aunt March. She confided her fears for her father. When Laurie discovered that Jo loved books as much as he did, he invited her to tour the spectacular house and, of course, to stop at the fabulous library. In the midst of their tour, a bell rang.

Jo said, "It must be your grandfather!"

"Don't tell me you're afraid of him?" Laurie asked.

"Maybe a little, but I don't know why."

The maid came in and told Laurie the doctor had arrived. While Laurie was being examined in another room, Jo stayed in the library and stood in front of a fine portrait of the elder Mr. Laurence.

Thinking she was alone, she said in a loud whisper, "I shouldn't be scared of him, for he's got kind eyes, though his mouth is a little grim and he looks like he must have tremendous will. He isn't as handsome as my grandfather, but I like him."

"Well thank you, young lady," said a voice from behind her. And there stood old Mr. Laurence! Well, poor Jo blushed until she couldn't blush any longer. For a minute, she thought she'd run away, but remained. Another look at the old man showed her that his eyes were even kinder than the painted ones.

After a very long pause, the old gentleman asked gruffly, "So you're not afraid of me?"

Jo said softly, "Not much, sir."

"But you do like me despite my bad features?"

Jo replied, "Oh yes, sir!"

Mr. Laurence was pleased with her answer and made Jo happy by saying that she had her grandfather's spirit. She explained that she came over to be neighborly, and they agreed that Laurie needed cheering up. She put her arm through Mr. Laurence's, and they joined Laurie in the parlor for tea. Soon, Jo and Laurie were again chatting like old friends, and Mr. Laurence decided she was a very good influence on the boy.

Jo admired the grand piano. After tea, she persuaded Laurie to play, and she only wished that Beth could have heard. Jo gushed about how well Laurie played until his grandfather stopped the compliments and gave her a rushed good-bye.

When they got to the front hall, Jo asked if she had done something to upset Mr. Laurence. Laurie said that his grandfather didn't like to hear him play the piano. He would tell her the reason another time. They promised to visit each other again.

Jo sprinted home to tell her family about the wonderful day she had being a good neighbor. Now, each of her sisters had a different reason to explore the house next door. Meg wanted to see the greenhouse. Amy was interested in the fine paintings and statues. And Beth longed to play the grand piano. Jo had made a good friend in Laurie, and was happy she had made him feel so much better.

∽

Beth called the big house "Palace Beautiful," though it took her some time to get up the nerve to visit. She was still afraid of old Mr. Laurence, even though he had put the other girls at ease. At first, they were shy because they couldn't repay material favors. But in a matter of weeks, they had forgotten their pride, and the friendship between Laurie and the March sisters grew full like grass in the spring.

Laurie told his tutor, Mr. Brooke, that the girls were all splendid. He often missed his lessons so he could go off with them. Laurie had never had a mother or sisters, and he rejoiced in the comfort and fun of the girls' companionship. Luckily, his grandfather thought this was a good idea and told Mr. Brooke not to worry if Laurie missed a lesson or two. He said, "Let him take a holiday! He needs good friends and exercise. I think I've been coddling him too much lately anyway."

What fun the group had! They skated, went on sleigh rides, made music, and put on plays. Soon everyone, except shy Beth, treated the Laurence mansion like a second home. Just as they anticipated, Meg often went to the greenhouse, Jo browsed in the library, and Amy copied the paintings. But, as much as she longed to, Beth couldn't find the courage to go next door and play the grand piano.

A little birdie named Jo had told Mr. Laurence about Beth's love of music. He set about to help her overcome her shyness. While visiting Marmee one day, he rambled on about the great musicians and wonderful singers he had seen. This coaxed Beth out of her corner, and she stood listening. Still pretending he didn't notice the timid little girl, he said, "Laurie neglects his music these days. That wonderful piano just sits there, dying to be used. If your girls want to practice on it, just to keep it in tune, I'd be grateful."

Beth stepped forward with her hands clasped tightly in excitement.

Mr. Laurence smiled and continued, "They needn't see anyone and no one would bother them. So please let the girls know what I've said, if any of them would care."

Beth slipped her little hand in his and

exclaimed, "Oh! They do care very much, sir!"

"Are you the musical girl?" he asked.

"I'm Beth. I love music very much, and I'll come to play the piano if you're sure that I won't bother anyone."

Mr. Laurence replied, "The house sits empty most afternoons. There's no chance you will bother anyone. So come and play as much as you like. It would make me very happy."

Beth blushed. She was still scared, but felt much better. She squeezed Mr. Laurence's hand because she had no words to thank him for his precious gift.

The old man stroked her hair and kissed her forehead. He said, in a soft voice, "I once had a little girl with eyes like yours. Bless you."

After a hasty good-bye to Mrs. March, Mr. Laurence left. Beth was ecstatic. She ran right upstairs to tell her dolls what had happened, because her sisters weren't home.

The next day, Beth watched as both Laurie and his grandfather left their house. After two or three tries, she finally managed to get herself into the mansion. She slipped quietly into the parlor room and stood in awe, staring at the beautiful piano. Someone had left music on the piano. With trembling fingers, she finally touched the great instrument, and her fear washed away. She sat down and played to her heart's content until Hannah came to take her home for dinner.

After this experience, Beth came to play the piano nearly every day. She never suspected that Mr. Laurence left new songs and exercise books for her, that he opened his study door to listen, or that Laurie made sure that no one interrupted her. She was so grateful for this blessing that she asked her mother if she could make Mr. Laurence a pair of slippers in thanks.

Of course, Mrs. March agreed. Meg and Jo helped choose the pattern and materials, and

Beth began the work. She was a very good seamstress, and the slippers were done in no time. She wrote a short note, and got Laurie to smuggle the slippers onto his grandfather's study table one morning so he could see them when he woke up.

Beth waited to see what would happen. Two days passed and she still heard nothing, so she worried that she might have upset her friend. On the afternoon of the second day, Beth went to run an errand. When she returned, her sisters and Hannah were excitedly waiting by the front door.

"Come, quickly, there's a letter for you!" Jo said.

Amy began, "Oh Beth! He's sent . . ." Jo clamped her hand over Amy's mouth, not wanting her to ruin the wonderful surprise.

When Beth stepped into the parlor, she

paled with both delight and surprise. Standing in front of her was a little cabinet piano with a letter on top addressed to "Miss Elizabeth March."

Beth gasped, "For me?" She held tightly to Jo for fear she might faint on the spot.

"Yes! It's for you," Jo squealed. "Isn't it wonderful of him? He's the dearest old man in the world."

She tried to hand Beth the letter and the key for the piano, but Beth shook her head. She was too excited, so Jo opened it and read: "Miss March, I've had many slippers in my life, but none that have suited me as well as yours. I want to give you something in return. This once belonged to the little granddaughter whom I lost. Great thanks and best wishes. Your friend, James Laurence."

"What an honor!" Jo said. "Laurie told me how fond Mr. Laurence was of his granddaughter who had died, and how he took such care of her things. Now, he's given you her piano!"

Only after Beth sat down to play the instrument did she feel better. Everyone exclaimed that it was the most remarkable piano they had ever heard—and how wonderful the girls felt watching their beloved sister lovingly touch the beautiful keys and press the shiny pedals!

"You'll have to thank him," Jo said, not thinking shy Beth would ever do such a thing.

"Yes. I guess I'll go now before I get too scared."

Much to the shock of her family, a miracle happened. Beth walked out the door, through the garden, and into the Laurence house. Then she marched in and knocked on the study door.

A gruff voice called out, "Come in!"

Beth went to Mr. Laurence, held out her hand, and said with a quivering voice, "I came to say thank you . . ." But she couldn't finish. He looked so kind and friendly that she threw her arms around his neck. She thought about the little girl he had lost and kissed his cheek.

Mr. Laurence was so touched by Beth's warmth that all his crustiness melted away. He set her upon his knee as if he had his granddaughter back again. Beth lost her fears and spoke to him as if she had known him her whole life. When she went home, he walked her to the door, shook her hand, and smiled as he tipped his hat in an elegant good-bye gesture.

Her sisters couldn't believe the performance. Jo danced a jig, Amy nearly fell out of the window as she watched, and Meg exclaimed, "I do believe the world is coming to an end!"

# CHAPTER 6

# Amy's Valley of Humiliation

～

Amy always used the wrong words. It was one of her most endearing quirks. One day, Laurie rode by on horseback. She watched and then proclaimed that he was the "perfect Cyclops."

"What do you mean?" Jo asked. "He's got two handsome eyes!" She resented anyone saying mean things about her dear friend.

Amy retorted, "I didn't say anything about his eyes. I was just admiring his riding."

Jo laughed out loud. "You meant to say 'centaur.'"

Amy didn't like Jo's teasing. She sulked for a minute about the misspoken word, and then said quietly, "I wish I had a little of the money that Laurie spends on that horse."

Meg asked, "Why?"

Amy admitted she was in a lot of debt. She owed at least a dozen pickled limes to her school-mates. Meg tried to be sympathetic and asked if limes were the fashion at school these days.

Amy explained how the limes were traded between friends for pencils, beads, and paper dolls. If a girl likes you, it's considered a great honor if she gives you a lime. If she doesn't favor you, then she'll just eat one in front of your face. "I've had so many, but I haven't returned them and I really should."

Meg took out her purse and gave Amy money to buy the limes. Amy thanked her profusely. Now she could show the girls at school that she was a good, fashionable friend.

Amy was late for school the next day because she stopped to buy twenty-five delicious limes. At school, when word got around, Amy's friends showered her with attention. Even Jenny Snow, who had made very mean remarks about Amy's "limeless" state, was nice to Amy. Not that it mattered, for Amy never forgot a slight. She promptly informed Jenny that she wouldn't be getting any of her treasures.

That morning, a special visitor to school praised Amy's beautifully drawn maps. When Amy puffed up like a proud peacock, Jenny became jealous. No sooner had the guest left than Jenny told the teacher, Mr. Davis, that Amy had pickled limes in her desk.

Now, Mr. Davis had outlawed limes, threatening a swift punishment to anyone who disobeyed him. He was a good teacher but didn't understand little girls. He had no patience for manners or upset feelings. On top of that, he had woken up on the wrong side of the bed that morning. So, when he heard the word "limes" from Jenny's lips, anger seeped into his stern face.

"Young ladies, your attention please!"

A hush fell upon the room as all fifty girls stared at the teacher.

"Miss March, come here please."

Amy rose, but felt afraid since she had broken the rules.

"Bring the limes that you have under your desk!"

Now even more scared, Amy shook out half a dozen limes into her desk and took the rest to Mr. Davis. She hoped he would relent when he smelled their delicious aroma, but Mr. Davis hated the smell. It only added to his anger.

"Is that all of them?"

Amy stammered, "Not quite."

"Bring the rest immediately."

Amy obeyed.

"Are you sure there are no more?" Mr. Davis asked.

"I never lie, sir."

"Fine. Now take these disgusting things and throw them out the window."

The entire class gasped. The promise of a special treat was forever lost. Burning with shame, Amy made a dozen trips to and from the window, each time tossing her plump, juicy limes onto the street.

When she finished, the teacher said, "Hold out your hand, Miss March."

Amy was startled. She had been one of Mr. Davis's favorites and hoped that he would not go any further in his punishment. She put her hands behind her, and, before she knew it, a soft hiss escaped her lips. Further irritated, Mr. Davis repeated, "Your hand, Miss March!"

A proud Amy threw her head back, held out her palm, and received the blows without flinching. This was the first time in her life she had been struck, and Amy felt the disgrace deeply within her proud little soul.

"Now, stand on the platform until recess."

How dreadful! To face the whole school, friends and enemies alike, with fresh shame seemed almost too hard to bear. Fixing her eyes on the stove at the back of the room, Amy stood still and took her punishment. Her heart ached, her hand stung, but nothing hurt as much as the thought of going home, telling her family, and facing their disappointment.

The fifteen minutes seemed like a lifetime. When recess was called, Amy gave Mr. Davis an indignant look that he wouldn't forget. She marched to the back of the room, gathered her things, and left for home, vowing never to return.

For the rest of the morning, Amy was inconsolable. She was still upset in the afternoon when

her mother and sisters arrived home. They tended to Amy's sore hand and wounded soul. Even old Hannah proclaimed Mr. Davis a "villain."

At school, no one noticed that Amy had left hours ago until Jo appeared with a note from Mrs. March. She took the rest of her sister's things and left.

From now on, Mrs. March told Amy, she could study at home with Beth.

"That's good! I wish everyone could leave and ruin his school. Oh, to think of those beautiful limes."

Marmee replied, "You did break the rules and deserved to be punished."

Amy cried, "Do you mean you're happy at the way I was disgraced?"

"No, of course not. I don't think teachers should hit children. But you are becoming conceited and you need to remember how to be modest."

"Exactly!" Laurie cried. He had been in the corner playing chess with Jo. "I once knew a girl who had great musical talent and composed delightful songs. She never knew how good she was."

Beth thought for a second. "I wish I knew such a girl. Maybe she could help me!"

Laurie said, "You do know her, and she helps you better than anyone." His dark eyes sparkled with mischief. Beth blushed terribly when she realized he was talking about her. Jo let him win the game as payment for his praise of her shy sister. Later, no amount of prodding could get Beth to play the piano. Laurie sang and played instead.

After he left, Amy asked why Laurie wasn't conceited, despite all his fine achievements. Mrs. March replied that even though Laurie was very accomplished, he used his talents modestly. Amy thought long and hard over this comment, taking it very much to heart.

# CHAPTER 7

# Jo Meets Her Match

Meg and Jo were getting ready for an evening out. Their bedroom was strewn with gloves, scarves, and hairpins.

Amy came in and asked, "Where are you going?"

Jo snapped, "Never mind. Little girls shouldn't ask questions."

Amy still wanted to know, so she turned to the more easygoing Meg. "Please tell me. Beth is playing with her dolls. I don't have anything to do. Let me come, too!"

Meg replied, "I can't take you because you weren't invited."

Jo added, "Stop whining! You simply can't come."

"You're going somewhere with Laurie, aren't you?"

Meg nodded. "Yes. Now, please stop bothering us."

Amy sat quietly for a minute. Then, she saw Meg slip a fan into her pocket and gasped, "I know! You're going to the theater!"

Jo became very angry and annoyed.

Amy didn't care. "I'll go, too. I've got my pocket money, and Mother said I could see the play in town." She took a deep breath. "It was very mean not to tell me."

Meg explained softly, for she had a special bond with Amy, "Mother doesn't want you to go tonight because you're not well. You'll see it next week with Beth and Hannah."

Amy cried, "But that's not as much fun as going with you and Jo and Laurie. I've been sick with this cold for so long. I'm dying to have some fun."

Meg turned to Jo. "Well, what if she does come? We can bundle her up."

Jo stood firm. "I'm not going if she goes! And if I don't go, Laurie won't like it. He invited only us two, not Amy. I would hope she'd think twice about poking in where she isn't wanted."

Jo's anger made Amy even more determined to get her way. She began to pull on her boots. "I am going. Meg just said I could!"

"And where will you sit?" Jo retorted. "We've got reserved seats!"

Amy began to cry. Meg tried to comfort her. Laurie called from outside and said it was time to go. Amy wailed on and on. She forgot all of her grown-up airs and acted like a spoiled baby. As Meg and Jo were stepping out the front door,

Amy called over the banister, "You'll be sorry for this, Jo March!"

"Fiddlesticks!" Jo yelled back, slamming the door. Once again, Jo's fiery spirit was at odds with Amy's stubborn will.

When they got back home after the play, Amy was reading in the parlor and refused to speak to them. Jo checked to make sure everything was all right in her room. The last time she and Amy fought, the younger sister had thrown Jo's dresser drawers upside down on the floor. Now, everything seemed normal. Jo decided that Amy had forgiven and forgotten.

But Jo was mistaken. The next day, the young author burst into the living room yelling, "Has anyone taken my book of stories?"

Both Meg and Beth immediately answered, "No."

Jo turned to her youngest sister, who was poking the fire. "Amy—you have it! You must."

"No, I don't."

"You know where it is then."

"No, I don't."

Jo cried, "You're lying!" She grabbed her sister by the shoulders.

"No! I'm not. I don't know where it is and I don't care."

Jo shook her sister a little. "You'd better tell me the truth!"

"Get as mad as you like. You'll never see your old stories again."

Jo looked extremely upset. "Why not?"

"I've burned them in the fire."

"You did *what*?" Jo turned very pale and clamped her hands even harder on Amy's shoulders. "My book that I've worked on for *years*? The one I intended to finish before Father gets home? Have you really *burned* it?"

"Yes, I did! I told you I would make you pay for—"

Jo's temper exploded. She shook her sister so hard that Amy's teeth chattered. "You wicked, wicked girl! I can never write it again. It's lost forever. I will never forgive you as long as I live. Never!"

Meg flew to rescue Amy from Jo's grip. Beth tried to pacify Jo, but she was too upset. She gave Amy a final punch on the ear and ran upstairs to the attic to be alone in her misery.

Jo's book of fairy-tale stories was her pride and joy. In her heart of hearts, Jo was simply inconsolable.

Dinner proved almost unbearable for the family. Jo was grim. Mrs. March had explained to Amy what a terrible thing she had done. Even Meg and Beth agreed. The little girl now felt terrible and wanted nothing more at that moment than to be forgiven. With all her heart she begged, "Please Jo, forgive me. I'm so very sorry."

Jo looked at Amy with fire in her eyes. "I will

*never* forgive you!" She then stopped talking to Amy.

Everyone felt the tension. Beth played the piano but Jo stood silently and Amy cried. Marmee went to kiss Jo good night and whispered, "Don't go to bed angry, my dear. Please try to forgive her." Jo wanted to cry but she winked away the tears and said loud enough for Amy to hear, "It was a horrible thing to do and she doesn't deserve to be forgiven."

Jo woke up feeling like a thundercloud. Amy wasn't any happier, making sarcastic remarks about unforgiving people. The bitter, winter day went badly for everyone.

After work, Jo didn't want to sit around the house. She decided to call on Laurie and go skating. Amy heard Jo getting her skates from the closet and whined to Meg, "She promised to take me! I guess there's no point in asking now."

Meg replied, "Well, you *were* very bad. Jo

worked very hard on her stories. She has a right to be upset." Meg put down her sewing. "But she might forgive you after Laurie's had a chance to calm her down. You could follow them, give Jo a kiss at the right moment, and everything could be okay."

Amy took Meg's advice to heart and chased after Jo and Laurie. Both were ready to skate well before Amy arrived. Jo saw her sister coming and turned her back. Laurie didn't see Amy because he was testing the ice. He called back to Jo, "Stay close to the edges—I think the middle might not be safe!"

Jo heard Amy struggle with her skates, but never turned around. She skated down the river, taking bitter satisfaction in knowing that Amy was having such a hard time. Jo had heard another of Laurie's warnings, but Amy hadn't. The angry part of Jo didn't care that Amy might be in danger. Amy skated toward the middle of the river. Jo turned around just in time to see her sister fall right through the ice. For a split second, Jo couldn't move. Laurie saw what happened and yelled, "Quick! Bring a rail!" Jo did exactly as Laurie said. They both worked hard to get a more-frightened-than-hurt Amy out of the water.

Laurie said, "We've got to get her home as quickly as possible. Let's wrap our coats around her to keep her warm."

Shivering, dripping, and crying, Amy made it home with their help. Soon, she was bundled in blankets before a hot fire. Jo raced around trying to make Amy comfortable. She didn't even notice that her dress was badly torn or that her hands were cut and bruised.

Later, Marmee tended to Jo's sore hands. Jo sobbed, feeling awful thinking that it would have been her fault if something terrible had happened to Amy. "How do I cure my temper? It just gets the best of me."

Marmee kissed Jo's wet cheek, saying, "My temper used to be just like yours. I've been trying to cure it for forty years, and have only succeeded in controlling it."

Knowing that her mother suffered the same burden lifted Jo's spirits. Marmee told Jo that it's far more rewarding to deal with anger sensibly and to be patient and have a good heart. They held each other tightly. Jo at once felt better.

Amy stirred from her cocoon.

Jo said, "I let myself stay angry. If it hadn't been for Laurie, Amy might have died. How could I be so wicked?"

Amy opened her eyes and held out her arms with a smile that went straight to Jo's heart. They didn't say a word. They hugged each other close, and all was forgiven and forgotten in one hearty kiss.

# CHAPTER 8

# Meg Goes to Vanity Fair

∽

April was upon their sleepy town and the weather had finally lifted. Meg was getting ready to spend two weeks at Annie Moffat's. The King children had come down with measles, so Meg would be getting an unplanned holiday. At first, Mrs. March had been hesitant to allow Meg to visit with the Moffats, but Sallie Gardiner promised to take good care of Meg. And now, Meg's sisters were helping her get ready.

"A whole two weeks of fun will be wonderful!" Jo exclaimed as she folded Meg's skirts.

Beth added, "You're lucky the weather has turned so lovely." She was sorting through neck and hair ribbons.

Amy sighed, "I wish I could have a good time and wear such nice clothes."

"I wish you were all coming with me," said Meg. "I'll keep all my adventures to tell you when I get back. It's the least I can do when you're all helping me so much."

Jo asked, "What did Mother give you from the treasure chest?"

"A pair of silk stockings, that pretty covered fan, and a lovely blue sash. I wanted the violet silk dress, but there wasn't time to alter it."

Meg had also borrowed all of her sisters' loveliest items. But she was still disappointed that her wardrobe was so old-fashioned and longed for the finery of more well-to-do girls. She lamented, "I wonder if a time will ever come when I have real lace on my clothes and bows on all my caps."

Beth reminded Meg that yesterday she had been happy just to be invited to Annie Moffat's house.

"You're right, Beth. I did say that and I *am* happy." Meg glanced at her trunk, which cheered her up. She said, "Everything's ready except my ball dress. Mother is going to fix it for me." Even though the old, white dress had been mended many times, it still made Meg happy.

Early the next morning, wearing her best traveling clothes, Meg left for her two-week vacation. When she arrived, she felt out of place in the Moffats' splendid house with its elegant, stylish occupants. The Moffats were good, kind people, despite their frivolous lifestyle. Soon, Meg realized that they were not very sophisticated underneath all their finery, and she felt right at home. She fell into a happy pattern of eating well, riding in a fine carriage, wearing her best dresses, and doing nothing but enjoying herself. She imitated the fashions of the day just like the other girls. She put on airs, used French phrases, and curled her hair. The more Meg saw of Annie Moffat's pretty things, the more she envied her.

However, Meg didn't have a lot of time for self-pity. She was too busy having fun. The girls shopped, walked, rode, and visited friends. They went to the theater or opera, or frolicked at home in the evening.

Annie's older sisters were delightful and accomplished. One, Belle, was even engaged, which Meg thought was very romantic. Mr. and Mrs. Moffat took a great liking to the young March girl, just as their daughter had. They called her "Daisy" and paid her many compliments. She soon got used to all the attention.

When the evening of the first formal party came, all the other girls were wearing new gowns. Meg pulled out her own ball gown, which looked old and shabby in comparison. No one said a word, but Meg's pride prickled and her cheeks burned with shame. Sallie, Annie, and Belle did her hair and helped tie her sash. They even praised her pretty, white arms. Meg felt they were just pitying her for being so poor.

Her heart felt heavy until the maid came in with a box of beautiful flowers. Annie quickly opened the lid. Soon all the girls were admiring the pretty roses. Annie said, "They're for Belle, I'm sure! Her fiancé always sends her flowers."

The maid said, "The flowers are for Miss March." She handed the note to Meg. The girls fluttered around Meg, asking questions.

"The note is from Mother, and the flowers are from Laurie," Meg said, slipping it into her pocket. Marmee's loving words improved her spirits, and she was so happy that Laurie hadn't forgotten her. She put aside a few flowers for herself, and then made little bouquets for her friends. She was so happy, she almost forgot about her shabby dress.

That evening, Meg danced to her heart's content. She had a grand time until she overheard a conversation that made her very upset.

A voice asked, "How old is he?"

Another responded, "Sixteen or seventeen, I think."

"It would be a good thing for one of those girls, don't you think? Sallie says they all get along so well, and the old man just dotes on them."

"Mrs. March has laid her plans. She'll play her cards right, even if it's a bit early for Meg to get married." Though she spoke softly, Meg recognized Mrs. Moffat's voice.

"She blushed when the flowers came, and then pretended she hadn't expected the note. It's a shame. She could be quite pretty if only she were more stylish. Do you think we could lend her a dress for Thursday?"

"She is proud, but that dowdy dress is all she has to wear."

"I'm going to ask that Laurence boy to come as a favor to Meg."

By the time Meg's partner arrived with her drink, she was flushed and feeling very agitated. Her pride helped hide her anger. She tried to forget the conversation she had just heard, but it kept replaying in her head. She desperately wanted to rush home and talk to her sisters, and to ask her mother for advice. Neither option was possible, so she did her best to appear happy and make it through the evening. And she was successful; no one suspected that she was acting.

When the party was over and she was in her room, she cried a little. She lay awake for a long while thinking hard about what had happened.

The next morning, Meg had a heavy heart and puffy eyes. Her vacation mood had drastically changed. She knew she should have spoken out and set the record straight last night. As the girls sat sewing that afternoon, they treated Meg with an air of respect. She was both surprised and flattered.

Belle said, "Daisy, I've invited your friend Mr. Laurence to the party on Thursday. We'd like to get to know him better. We thought it would also be a great favor for you."

Meg blushed. She thought for a second, and said, "You're so kind. He probably won't come."

Belle asked, "Why not?"

Meg replied, "He's too old!"

"How old is he?"

"Why, nearly seventy." Meg tried hard not to laugh.

Belle giggled, "You goose, we meant the young man!"

"There isn't any," Meg said. "Laurie's only a boy."

The sisters exchanged strange looks. Annie said, "He's about your age, isn't he?"

Meg replied, "Not really. He's more my sister Jo's age. I'm going to be seventeen in August."

Annie said, "But he sent you those flowers?"

Meg replied, "He does things like that all the time for my family. My mother and his grandfather are old friends. It's quite natural for us to play together." She hoped that would put the matter to rest.

Annie whispered to Belle, "She's very innocent, isn't she?"

Mrs. Moffat came into the room to ask if the girls needed anything. Sallie said her clothes were all set for Thursday. Meg said the same thing even though she needed many new things she simply couldn't have.

After Mrs. Moffat left, Sallie asked, "What are you going to wear?"

Meg said, "My old white gown again if I can fix it for Thursday because I tore it last night."

Sallie said, "Why don't you send home for another?"

Meg swallowed her pride and answered, "I haven't got another."

Belle said, "No need to send home. You can borrow one of mine."

Meg smiled. "That's so kind, but my old dress suits me just fine."

The girls begged and pleaded until Meg agreed to borrow Belle's dress. She had forgotten all about last night's conversation.

On Thursday, Belle shut Meg inside her room. With the help of her maid, they transformed her into the height of fashion. They laced her into a tight, blue-silk dress. They curled her hair. They powdered her neck and arms, and would have applied rouge if Meg hadn't sternly declined. They added bracelets, a necklace, and earrings. Meg felt very unlike herself; she looked very beautiful.

Meg went downstairs in the high French heels, trying hard not to trip over the dress. Compliments poured from everyone. Sallie even told her how lovely she looked, trying not to be jealous.

The atmosphere at this party was completely different from that of the last one. Girls who refused to notice Meg before now paid her a great deal of attention. Young men, who before only stared, now asked to be introduced.

Mrs. Moffat was busy explaining Meg's identity to many of the older women. "Daisy March," she said. "Her father's a colonel in the army. She's from one of our first families. They've fallen upon hard times, but she's an intimate friend of the

Laurences. She's a very sweet girl. My Ned's quite taken with her."

Meg was shocked at Mrs. Moffat's bold lies. It was hard to act like she didn't hear the whispers and the conversations. She simply decided to have fun. She played her part well, even if her feet hurt from the shoes. She even flirted with a young man for a little while.

Suddenly, she saw Laurie arrive. He stared at her with surprise and disapproval. Belle and Annie gave one another knowing glances. This confused Meg even further. She decided to right the situation and greet Laurie.

"I was afraid you wouldn't come," she said.

"Jo wanted me to, so I could tell her how you looked."

Meg asked, "What will you say to her?"

"That you look very unlike yourself. You look so grown up that I'm a little afraid of you."

"That's silly," Meg said. "The girls dressed me

71

up for fun. Wouldn't Jo stare if she saw me now?"

"She sure would."

Meg's feelings were hurt. "You don't like me like this?"

"No, I don't."

"Why not?"

Laurie looked at her fine dress, bare shoulders, and curled hair. "I don't like fuss and feathers."

Well, this was too much coming from a boy younger than she was. Meg fumed, "You are the rudest boy ever!"

She walked to a window to cool off. Overhearing a nasty comment about her overdone outfit, she realized she should have worn her own clothes, rather then feel so uncomfortable and ashamed. She stood half hidden behind the curtains until Laurie came, held out his hand, and said, "Please forgive my rudeness and dance with me."

He explained that though he didn't like her dress, she did look lovely. She tried to act angry, but her favorite waltz was playing. They twirled merrily around and only stopped when Meg got out of breath.

"Laurie," she asked, "can you do me a favor?"

"Of course!"

"Please don't tell them at home about my dress tonight."

Laurie asked, "Why did you wear it if you are so ashamed?"

"I don't mind if they know, but I want to tell them myself." She paused, "I'll need to confess how I've been acting so silly."

Laurie nodded. "Well, what shall I say when they ask?"

"Just that I had a good time and that I looked nice."

Laurie looked concerned. "Are you really having a good time?"

"Not at this moment, no. I wanted a little fun, but now I'm getting tired of it."

Ned Moffat came to collect his three dances. Meg looked at Laurie and rolled her eyes. He laughed, knowing Meg meant that Ned was such a bore.

Laurie didn't catch sight of Meg until after dinner when she was drinking champagne with Ned and his friend Fisher. Both boys were acting like fools. Ned went to get another drink and Fisher left to retrieve Meg's fan.

Laurie whispered to Meg, "You'll have a splitting headache tomorrow if you drink too much. Your mother might not like it."

She replied, "I'm not Meg tonight. I'm a doll who does crazy things. Tomorrow I'll be back to my old self and put away all my fuss and feathers."

For the rest of the evening, Laurie watched Meg dance, laugh, chatter, and flirt. He was embarrassed by her behavior and would have said something, but Meg avoided him until it was time to say good night.

"Not a word!" She put her finger to her lips.

Laurie replied solemnly, "On my honor."

All the girls were curious to hear about Laurie, but Meg was too tired and her head ached. She was glad Saturday was only two days away. She couldn't wait to go home, feeling very used up after two weeks of fun.

Meg told her sisters all about her adventures when she got home. On Sunday, after Beth and Amy had gone to bed, she sat quietly by the fire.

"Home is a wonderful place, even if it isn't splendid."

Marmee said, "I'm so glad to hear you say that, Meg. I was afraid home would feel dull after your fine accommodations."

Meg thought for a minute, and then said, "Marmee, I have to confess."

She told her mother and Jo everything that happened at the Moffats' party, including the fancy dress and the champagne. She said that she knew Laurie was disappointed by her behavior. She described her flirting with the boys and the gossip she had overheard.

Marmee's lips turned white. Jo exclaimed, "Well, that's just nonsense. Why didn't you tell them so?"

Meg looked down. "I felt ashamed and embarrassed. Then, it just made me angry."

Jo exclaimed, "Imagine us being nice to Laurie and his grandfather just so he'll marry one of us—how silly." She laughed. The next time she saw Annie Moffat, she vowed, she'd give her a piece of her mind.

Marmee quietly told Jo that gossip must never be repeated, but forgotten as soon as possible. She did have plans for them, but they weren't at all like the ones Mrs. Moffat had outlined. She wanted her girls to grow up and be accomplished and good—to be admired, respected, and lead useful, pleasant lives. She wanted them to find love, but never to marry just for the sake of a fortune.

She added, "Be patient, and leave these things to time. Everything will work out exactly as it should." With that piece of excellent advice, both girls went up to bed with untroubled thoughts and hopeful hearts.

# CHAPTER 9

# Experiments

~ஓ

On a warm June day, Meg came home and excitedly announced: "The Kings are off to the seashore tomorrow. I'm free! Three whole months of vacation!"

Jo had collapsed on the sofa, Beth took off her dusty boots, and Amy made lemonade for everyone. Then Jo said, "Aunt March went to Plumfield today. I was so afraid she'd ask me to go with her. The very minute she was in the carriage, I ran all the way home."

Beth cuddled Jo's feet. "Poor Jo. She came running in like bears were after her!"

"Aunt March is a regular samphire, isn't she?" Amy asked, sipping her lemonade.

Jo sighed, "She means *vampire*, but it's too hot to worry about wrong words today."

Amy changed the subject. "What will you do on your vacation?"

Meg thought for a second. "I'm going to lie in bed and do nothing!" she answered. "I've been getting up early all winter taking care of other people. This summer I'm going to be as lazy as I want."

"I'm going to read and read and read!" said Jo, "and spend time with Laurie."

Amy chimed in, "Let's forget about lessons, Bethy, and play all the time."

Beth replied, "That sounds like fun, if Mother says it's okay. There are new songs I want to learn. And my dolls all need new clothes."

Marmee was quietly sewing in her corner. Meg asked, "Oh, Mother, may we?"

Mrs. March replied, "You may try it for a week. I think by Saturday you'll find that all play and no work is as bad as all work and no play."

Meg sighed, "Oh, no! I'm sure it will be absolutely lovely."

Jo raised her glass: "A toast—fun forever and no work!"

They happily drank their lemonade and spent the rest of the day lying about the house.

The next day, nothing went as expected. No chores were done, and each sister had her own fun. But they weren't exactly pleased. Jo read until her eyes hurt so much that she quarreled with

Laurie. After an attempt to sketch outdoors, Amy got stuck in the rain and ruined her dress. Meg went shopping only to find that the material didn't wash well. Beth took everything out of the closet to build a new home for her dolls, but she got so tired she left it halfway through. At dinnertime they agreed that, despite the fun, the day seemed too long without some work to keep their idle hands busy.

By Friday, all four girls felt out of sorts. No one would admit that the experiment was failing. Mrs. March decided to have a bit of fun. She gave Hannah the day off, so when the girls got up on Saturday morning they found a cold kitchen with no breakfast. And Marmee was nowhere to be found.

"What's going on?" Jo exclaimed.

Meg ran upstairs. When she came back, she explained, "Mother's tired. She's going to rest today. We have to get along as best we can."

"Okay," Jo said. "I'm aching for something to do—I mean for a bit of excitement."

It was a relief to have some work. The younger girls set the table as Jo and Meg made breakfast.

Meg brought a tray up to Marmee. It contained bitter tea, soggy biscuits, and a burned omelet. Once Meg left, Marmee had a good laugh. "Poor souls," she thought. "They'll have a hard time, but it'll be good for them."

Everyone complained about the awful breakfast. For the next meal, Jo decided to do the cooking. Meg reluctantly agreed after making such a mess of things.

Jo invited Laurie for lunch to make up for their quarrel. With perfect faith in her abilities, she chose a menu and made a shopping list. There was only one problem. She had no idea how to cook. Meg said she'd help if necessary, even though she didn't know how to make much more than a loaf of bread. With Marmee going out for lunch, Jo was pretty much on her own.

All of a sudden, Jo heard Beth crying in the living room. She rushed in to find her sister sobbing over Pip, her canary, who lay dead in his cage. They hadn't fed him. Beth removed the bird from the cage and cried, "Oh, Pip! How could I be so cruel? I forgot all about you."

Jo said, "We'll give him a proper funeral after lunch. Don't cry, Bethy. It's been a strange week. Poor Pip just got the worst of it."

She left Beth in the warm arms of Meg and Amy and went back to the kitchen. She reset the fire and piled up the dishes. While the water was heating, she walked to the market and bought a young lobster, asparagus, and two boxes of very tart strawberries.

When she got home, she discovered Meg had forgotten about the bread. It had soured, but Jo had to bake it anyhow. She labored through her preparations until everything was done.

Lunch proved to be an even bigger disaster than breakfast. Jo overcooked the asparagus, burned the bread, undercooked the potatoes, and mutilated the lobster. The cake was lumpy and the cream was sour. And to make matters worse, she put salt on the berries instead of sugar! Jo almost cried right at the table. Laurie's eyes were twinkling, though, and Jo finally burst into a fit of laughter. And so did everyone else! Instead of the fancy lunch Jo had planned, they all dined on biscuits, butter, olives—and a bit of fun.

That afternoon they gave Pip a proper funeral.

Jo and Meg spent the rest of the day cleaning up the mess from the terrible meals. Beth wanted to lie down, only no beds had been made, so she spent the afternoon fluffing pillows and shaking out blankets.

Marmee arrived home and found all four of her daughters looking exhausted, frustrated, and more than a little fed up with their experiment.

"Well, my girls, are you satisfied with your week of all play, or do you need another week?"

Jo said decidedly, "I sure don't." Everyone echoed her words. Then Jo added, "All work and no play isn't for us, that's for sure!"

Meg asked, "Mother, did you go away today just to see how we would get along without you?"

Marmee smiled and nodded. She explained that a house runs well only when everyone helps. She asked, "Isn't it better to work hard so you can enjoy your leisure?"

The girls agreed. They had all learned a life-long lesson: that there is balance and harmony in both work and play.

# CHAPTER 10

## Camp Laurence

‹❧›

One July day Beth came into the house with her arms full of parcels. She was appointed mistress of the post office the two houses had set up for fun because she spent the most time at home.

One was a peculiar package that, after Meg opened it, revealed one letter and one glove.

"Why, where's the other one?" Meg remembered leaving a pair at Laurie's. Beth said she'd only found one in the post office.

"Oh, I hate odd gloves." Meg put down her

sewing and opened the letter. It was a translation of a German song. She said, "Mr. Brooke must have done this. It isn't Laurie's handwriting."

Marmee glanced at her pretty daughter. She had a brief thought about a brewing romance between Meg and Mr. Brooke. Meg had no idea what her mother was thinking. She was quite happy to sit sewing and singing.

Jo also had "mail." She laughed when Beth handed her a big, floppy hat. "I told Laurie the other day that I wished big hats were the fashion because I was always getting sunburned," Jo explained. "He said, 'Why care about fashion? Wear a big hat and be comfortable.' "

Jo also received a note from her mother, who was proud of how well she was controlling her temper. Another letter was from Laurie inviting everyone to a picnic: his friends, the Vaughns, were visiting from England.

Jo was excited. "Can we go, Marmee?" she asked. "Meg and I will be a great help and it'll be fun for Beth and Amy."

Meg asked, "Do you know anything about the Vaughns?"

Jo replied, "They're friends of Laurie's from abroad. Kate's older than you; the twins, Fred and Frank, are my age; and Grace is about nine."

"I'm so glad my French print is pressed!" Meg said, ever mindful of her fashion. "Jo, do you have something decent?"

Jo rolled her eyes and stated that her gray boating suit would do just fine. After all, she would be spending the day rowing and eating outdoors.

Beth said she was a bit afraid of the new boys, but she would love to go anyway. Jo encouraged her sisters to get their chores done so they could spend the holiday without a care in the world.

When Jo woke up the next morning, she

noticed with a laugh that Amy had a clothespin on her nose to uplift its shape no matter how much it hurt! The day was bright and beautiful, perfect for a picnic. All four girls got dressed. Beth finished first and went to the window to watch the bustling scene next door. "Oh, Laurie's dressed like a sailor," she reported to her sisters. "And Ned Moffat and Sallie Gardiner and Mr. Brooke are there, too. What fun, girls! What fun!"

Soon, all four were ready. Meg was mortified that Jo was wearing her big, floppy hat. They headed next door to meet Laurie's friends. He made polite introductions. Jo noticed that Kate was standoffish. "Perhaps that's why Laurie clams up when he's speaking of her," she thought.

Beth came out of her shell a little when she noticed that Frank walked with a cane. He was both kind and gentle. Soon, Amy was chumming around with little Grace as if they had known each other all their lives.

Mischief was underfoot within the two boats. Fred did his best to overturn them. Everyone had a good laugh at Jo's funny hat. Kate was amazed at Jo, who forgot herself and cried "Christopher Columbus!" when she lost her oar.

The big tent was set up by the time the party arrived at the picnic area. Laurie jumped out and announced in his jolly voice, "Welcome to Camp Laurence!" He then suggested they have a game of croquet before lunch. They divided into two teams. Jo had to control her temper when she caught Fred Vaughn cheating. In the end it didn't matter, because they all had a good time playing the game.

Next, it was time for lunch. Everyone helped. The younger campers gathered sticks for the fire. The older girls set the table. The boys got the fire going. The meal was lovely. They ate and ate. Laurie and Jo had to share a plate because one was missing.

"There's salt over there," Laurie said, "if you want it for your berries."

Jo laughed, "How dare you remind me of that awful lunch when everything here is so perfect."

"It had nothing to do with me. You, Meg, and Mr. Brooke have done all the work." He paused for a minute. "What shall we do after lunch?"

Jo answered, "We'll play games in the tent until it's cooler. I've brought Authors, and I bet Kate knows some new games. You should really be paying more attention to her. She is your guest."

Laurie protested. He said Jo was also his guest. Plus, he thought Kate and Mr. Brooke would spend the afternoon together, but Mr. Brooke kept talking to Meg.

Jo gave him one of her looks. Finally, Laurie sighed, "Okay, I'm going."

The entire group settled into the tent to wait for the heat to pass. Jo was right: Kate did know some fun parlor games. They played Truth, Rigmarole, and then Authors. Afterward Kate, Meg, and Mr. Brooke left the younger children to play in the tent. Sitting on the grass, Kate began to sketch. Meg said longingly, "How beautiful! I wish I could draw."

Kate asked, "Why don't you learn?"

"I haven't the time."

"Why?" Kate asked in her British accent. "Is it because of school?"

Meg said, "Oh, I don't go. I'm a governess myself."

Kate's disapproving expression made Meg blush. Mr. Brooke explained, "American girls are very independent. They are admired for supporting themselves."

Kate didn't seem impressed, which made Meg feel even worse. Mr. Brooke turned to Meg and asked if she enjoyed the German song he translated for her.

Her face brightened. "Oh, yes, very much. Thank you."

The rest of the afternoon found Meg and Mr. Brooke engaged in a lovely conversation. A friendly game of croquet finished the day for the rest of the gang. At sunset, they took down the tent. They packed the gear, loaded the boats, and made their way home. Everyone proclaimed Camp Laurence a magnificent success!

# CHAPTER 11

## Castles in the Air

Laurie was swinging in his hammock on a warm September day. He wondered what his neighbors were doing, but he was too lazy to find out. He hadn't finished his studies, frustrating Mr. Brooke. Instead, he had practiced the piano, upsetting his grandfather. Then Laurie had played a practical joke on one of the maids and got into an argument with the stableman. Everyone in the house now seemed angry with him. Thankfully, he fell asleep, and a good nap improved his mood. The sound of voices woke him from a dream where he was having an adventure at sea. He opened his eyes to see the March sisters coming out of their house.

They looked odd. Each wore a large hat and carried a shoulder pouch and a tall walking stick. They marched through the garden and up the hill toward the river. Laurie felt slighted that they hadn't invited him. He decided to follow them.

He found the girls sitting in a shady nook. Meg was sewing, Amy was drawing pictures, Jo was knitting and reading aloud, and Beth was sorting pinecones. Laurie felt bad about spying, but he was so lonely that he approached them.

"May I come in?" he asked. "Or will I bother you?" Meg lifted her eyebrows.

Jo said, "Of course you can join us. I should have asked you to come, but I didn't know if you'd want to play our girls' games."

"I'm sure it'll be fun, but if Meg wants me to go, I will."

Meg said, "You may stay as long as you do something. This is our Busy Bee Society. It's against the rules to be idle here."

"What should I do?"

Jo handed him a book to read aloud while she knit the heel of her sock. When he finished, he asked, "What game are we playing?"

Meg asked her sisters, "Should we tell him?"

Amy warned, "He'll laugh!"

Laurie said, "No, I won't. I promise."

Jo explained how they had been trying all year to be good, productive girls. They'd bring their work to this spot, where they felt inspired by the view of the wide, blue river, the green hills, and the silvery white clouds shining like the steeples of a city in the sky. For fun, they'd wear old hats and play pilgrims on the way.

Jo sighed, "Wouldn't it be fun if all our 'castles in the air' came true?"

Laurie said it would be hard for him to follow

just one dream because he had so many different ones.

"Which one is your favorite?" Jo asked.

"I'll tell you mine if you all tell me yours!"

They all agreed.

Laurie said emphatically, "I'd live in Germany and become a famous musician. That's my 'castle.'" He turned to Meg. "Your turn."

She stated, "I'd like to be mistress of a beautiful house and manage it very well."

Laurie teased, "With a wonderful husband?"

Meg blushed. Jo said bluntly, "Your castle wouldn't be perfect without a good husband and little angels for children, and you know it!"

Meg retorted, "Well, you'd have nothing but horses, pens and ink, and novels in yours!"

Jo smiled. "Exactly! I'd write and become as famous from my stories as Laurie would be from his music."

Beth quietly noted, "My dream is to stay

home with Mother and Father and help take care of the family."

Laurie asked, "Is that all?"

"Yes," Beth said, "now that I've got my little piano, that's all I need."

Amy piped up, "My dream is to move to Rome and become a great artist."

Laurie said thoughtfully, "We're an ambitious group. Each wants to be rich and famous, except for Beth. I wonder if we'll all succeed."

Jo said, "I've got the key to my castle, but whether I can unlock it is another story."

"Me too," Laurie sighed.

Amy held up her pencil. "And here's my key!"

Meg said softly, "I haven't got any."

Laurie responded, "Oh, yes you do. You have your pretty face." This caused Meg to blush again. "Wait and see," he said, "if it doesn't bring you something worthwhile."

Jo suggested, "Let's meet here in ten years and

see how well we've done." Everyone said this was indeed a fine plan.

Laurie remarked thoughtfully, "I hope I've done something to be proud of by then, but I'm so lazy."

Jo said soothingly, "All you need is some inspiration."

Laurie said, "I should be happy to please my grandfather. He wants me in the family business, but I want to be a musician. And I really want to see the world."

Jo suggested, "You should sail away and only come back after you've tried your own way."

Meg scolded, "That's not right. Laurie, you should do as your grandfather wants. Once he sees that you're doing your best in college, he'll be sure to grant your wishes." She continued, "Do your duty and you'll be respected and admired like Mr. Brooke."

Laurie asked what Meg knew about him.

"That he took care of his mother until she died and now provides for his mother's old nurse."

Laurie agreed that Mr. Brooke was a fine man. Meg went on to tell Laurie that he should also listen to his tutor and do well in his studies. Laurie was offended for a minute, but regained his good humor.

The Busy Bee Society got back to work. Laurie tried twice as hard to be good to ensure his membership.

That night, while Beth played the piano for his grandfather, Laurie watched quietly from the doorway. He thought hard about what Meg had said, and vowed to himself, "I'll let my castle go for now—and stay with my dear grandfather while he needs me, for I am all he has."

# CHAPTER 12

# Secrets

ᖚ

October came with chilly weather and shorter afternoons. Hidden under an old blanket, Jo scribbled away in the attic while Scrabble played at her feet. She dotted her last sentence, signed her name with a flourish, and exclaimed, "There! I've done my best."

Then, she tied up the bundle with red ribbon and removed a second manuscript from its secret hiding place. She put them both in her pocket and crept quietly downstairs.

Jo snuck out of the house and took the long

way into town. Once at her destination, she tried several times to go inside. There was a dentist's sign on the building's entrance. On her third try, she made it up the dusty stairs. By chance, Laurie was across the street and saw Jo go inside. He crossed the street and waited under the sign. He said to himself, "It's just like Jo to come alone. If she has a bad time, I can walk her home."

In ten minutes, Jo appeared with a red face, looking like she'd been through an ordeal. She wasn't happy to see Laurie and tried to walk past him, but he followed her.

He asked, "Was it awful?"

"Not really."

"Quick, though."

"Yes, thankfully."

He asked, "Why did you go by yourself?"

"I didn't want anyone to know."

Laurie chastised her. "You're so silly. How many did you have out?"

Jo laughed. She realized that Laurie thought she had been at the dentist's. Her eyes twinkled as she answered, "I have to wait a week for the two I want to come out."

Laurie asked, "Why are you laughing? What are you up to?"

Jo replied, "What are *you* up to? What were you doing in that pool hall?"

He explained that it wasn't a pool hall, but a gym. He had been taking fencing lessons.

"Oh!" Jo said, "that's fun! You can teach me, and we can play Hamlet."

It was Laurie's turn to laugh. He agreed to teach her even if they didn't play Hamlet. The walk back home was pleasant, except for one small disagreement. Jo warned Laurie about becoming a wild boy. She said that her mother wouldn't like it.

"Are you going to lecture me all the way home?"

Jo replied, "Of course not, why?"

"If you are, I'll make my way home. If not, I'd like to tell you a secret."

The prospect of an exciting secret was too much for Jo. "No more advice," she said. "Now, out with it!"

But Laurie wouldn't tell her until she explained what she had been doing in town. So Jo said that she had been at the newspaper office and left two of her stories with the editor. She had to wait a week to find out if they would be accepted.

Laurie yelled, "Hurrah for Miss March, the celebrated author!" He tossed his hat in the air.

She frowned. "Oh stop. He might not accept them, but I couldn't rest until I tried."

Laurie said that her stories were so good, they'd surely be published. Now, it was time for *his* secret. He said that he knew where to find Meg's lost glove, whispering that he saw it in Mr. Brooke's pocket. "Isn't it romantic?"

Jo scowled, "No. It's horrid." She hated the idea of someone taking Meg away from the family. "I don't think I like secrets. I'm upset now that you've told me."

Laurie wanted to make his friend feel better. "How about a race down the hill?"

They ran wildly down the slope. Jo's hat and hairpins dropped out along the way, but the burst of energy did the trick and cheered her right up. By the time she reached Laurie at the bottom of the hill, she was out of breath.

"I wish I was a horse, then I could run for miles and never get tired," she panted. "Will you be a dear and get my things?"

Jo tried to fix her hair before she met anyone on the path, but it was too late. Meg came along wearing her best dress. She took one look at her sister and said, "Jo, when will you stop running all about?"

Jo replied, "Not until I'm old and gray. Don't make me grow up before my time, Meg." She bit her lip to stop from crying. The secret sat in a dark pit at the bottom of her stomach. The last thing she wanted was for her sister to grow up and get married.

Laurie joined the conversation just in time. He asked Meg, "Where were you?"

"At the Gardiners'. Sallie was telling me all about Belle Moffat's wedding."

"Did it make you jealous?" Laurie asked.

Meg admitted, "I'm afraid it did."

"I'm happy about it," Jo muttered, jerking her hat strings. "If you care about riches, you will never marry a poor man."

Laurie's eyes widened. He didn't want his secret to fly out unannounced.

"I don't believe I shall ever marry," Meg said, and walked ahead of them. Jo and Laurie behaved like children, throwing rocks, laughing, and whispering. Meg was tempted to join them, but not in her best dress.

For a week, Jo acted very strangely. She rushed to the door whenever the postman came. She was often rude to Mr. Brooke and peered at Meg so oddly that the entire family was bewildered. On the next Saturday, Meg looked outside the window to see Laurie racing up to Jo in the garden. He was flapping a newspaper in his hands. Jo wrestled it from him and burst into the house. She dropped onto the sofa and pretended to read.

"Anything interesting?" Meg inquired.

Jo looked up. "Just a story."

Beth wanted to know what it was called.

Jo replied, " 'The Rival Painters.' "

Meg was curious. "Why don't you read it?"

The girls listened carefully as Jo cleared her throat and read at lightning speed. Each sister had a different compliment. Then, Amy asked who wrote it.

Suddenly Jo sat up and said, "Your sister!"

Squeals of delight followed. Each looked to see "Miss Josephine March" printed clearly. Jo was laughing and crying. To be independent and earn the praise of her loved ones were her dearest wishes.

# CHAPTER 13

# A Telegram

∽

The girls were in disagreeable moods on a dull November afternoon. Then Marmee arrived home and Laurie came over, cheering them a little.

Laurie asked, "I'm taking Mr. Brooke home. Does anyone want to come for a ride?"

Beth and Jo said they'd love to go.

"Is there anything I can do for you, Madam Mother?" Laurie asked Mrs. March.

Before Marmee could answer, the doorbell rang and Hannah entered the living room with a puzzled look. She said, "It's one of those horrid telegraph things, ma'am."

As Mrs. March quickly read it, her face turned white and she fell back into her chair. Laurie ran to get a glass of water as Jo read: "Mrs. March. Your husband is very ill. Come at once. S. Hale, Washington Hospital."

Suddenly, the family's whole world had changed. The terrible news shocked everyone. Mrs. March held the girls tightly as she said, "I'll go at once, but it may already be too late!"

Sounds of sobbing filled the room. The first to recover, Hannah sat up and said, "No more crying! I'll go get your things ready, ma'am."

Marmee said quietly, "She's right, girls. Let's be calm. I need to think."

Each girl tried her hardest to be calm.

Marmee was still pale, but stood steadily. She thought for a minute and then said, "Where's Laurie?"

"Right here," he said, hurrying from the next room. "How can I help?"

Marmee said, "Please send a telegram saying I will come at once. The next train to Washington leaves early in the morning."

Laurie nodded. "Is there anything else? The horses are ready. I can go anywhere or do anything!" He looked ready to fly to the moon if it would help.

Marmee replied, "Perhaps you could leave a note at Aunt March's? Jo, hand me a pen and paper."

Jo did as she was asked. She felt terribly helpless knowing that the money for the train trip would have to be borrowed from Aunt March. She wished that she could add something of her own.

With note in hand, Laurie rushed out the front door and down the street as if his life depended upon it. Soon, Marmee put the girls to work. Beth's job was to fetch old bottles of wine from Mr. Laurence for her father. The elderly gentleman came back with Beth, bringing everything he could think of for an invalid. He even asked if he could accompany Mrs. March. Knowing that Mr. Laurence was not fit for the long journey, Marmee thanked him and said that she would be fine on her own—even if she didn't feel that way. No one gave it a second thought when Mr. Laurence bid them a hasty good-bye. That is, until Meg answered the door to find Mr. Brooke.

"I've come to see if your mother will allow me to escort her to Washington," he said, lowering his lovely brown eyes.

Meg smiled warmly. "How kind you are. It will be such a relief for my mother. Thank you so much."

Laurie returned with the money from Aunt March. The girls kept as busy as possible under the awful circumstances. They all tried hard not to think about their father and held back their tears. As the afternoon wore on, Meg noticed that Jo was missing. She finally arrived, wearing a peculiar expression, then passed her mother a handful of bills, saying, "Here, that's my contribution."

Marmee gasped, "Jo! Where did you get twenty-five dollars?"

She answered, "Don't worry, Marmee. I earned it fair and square. I only sold what was mine." Then, Jo took off her hat to reveal that her long, wavy hair was cut short!

Marmee cried, "Your hair! Your beautiful hair!"

"I've sold it," said Jo. "It'll be good for me. I was becoming far too vain."

Amy sighed, "It was your best feature! What

made you do it?" She couldn't imagine such a sacrifice.

"I was desperate to help Father. That was all I could do."

Mrs. March looked lovingly at her daughter and said, "Thank you very much, my dearest."

# CHAPTER 14

## Hope and Faith

࿐

No one said much the next morning as they rose earlier than usual to a cold, gray day. They ate a quiet breakfast together. Their faces were grave as they waited for the carriage to take their mother to the station. Instructing the girls not to worry, Mrs. March told them to have hope and keep busy. All four took her advice to heart. They hugged Marmee close one last time before she and Mr. Brooke rode away.

When the carriage was quite out of view, the girls went back inside the house, remembering their new motto: "Hope and Keep Busy."

Jo and Meg returned to work. Amy and Beth stayed home to help Hannah. They found relief in their routine. News about their father was also a great comfort. Mr. Brooke sent a bulletin each day—and it seemed Father was truly getting better. The days flew by as fat letters were exchanged between their home and the hospital in Washington. The letters became a wonderful lifeline during this difficult time.

≈

Ten days had passed since Marmee left for Washington. While the girls were working hard to "hope and keep busy," they also took many breaks. That morning, Beth reminded Meg and Jo to go to the Hummels, for Mrs. March had asked them to look after the unfortunate family in her absence. Meg was too tired to go, and Jo was home from Aunt March's nursing a cold.

Jo said, "Why don't you go, Beth? The walk would do you good."

Beth replied, "My head aches and I'm very tired. I thought one of you would go today."

Meg suggested they wait for Amy, but she didn't come home. The older girls promptly forgot about the Hummels, so Beth quietly went out in the chilly air. No one noticed when she got home, either, for she simply walked upstairs to her mother's room and shut herself inside.

Jo came into the room and found her little sister looking terrible with red eyes. She exclaimed, "Christopher Columbus! What's the matter?"

Before Jo could come closer, Beth held out her hand and asked, "You've had scarlet fever, haven't you?"

Jo responded, "Yes. When Meg did. We were babies. Why?"

Through sobs, Beth told Jo that the Hummels' baby had died in her lap. The doctor had said it was scarlet fever, and told Beth to go right home and take the medicine because she also might get ill.

Jo hugged her sister close. "No, you can't be. If you get sick, I'll never forgive myself." She felt Beth's forehead and said, "Oh Beth! I'm so afraid you will get sick. You've been over there every day this week." Jo paused for a minute to gather Beth's hands in her own. "We need to call Hannah. She'll know what to do."

Hannah told Jo to get the doctor right away. Dr. Bangs came and said that Beth definitely had symptoms of the fever, though it would be a mild case. Everyone decided that Amy, who'd never had the illness, should move in with Aunt March. But it was only after a promise of daily visits from Laurie that Amy agreed to go. Jo would stay home and nurse Beth, because Amy could now attend to their aunt.

Amy almost burst into tears in Aunt March's parlor until Laurie pulled Polly the Parrot's tail and made her laugh. Once alone, she reflected, "I don't think I can bear it, but I'll try."

# CHAPTER 15

# Dark Days

༼ᔆ༽

The illness settled right into poor Beth. Hannah and the doctor took good care of her. Meg stayed home to keep up the house. Hannah gave strict instructions to the girls not to tell their mother anything. Their father had had a relapse, and Hannah didn't want anything else to upset his recovery. She had no doubt that Beth would soon get well.

Heavy hearts carried Jo and Meg through these dark days. They were both so afraid to think of life without their special little sister. Beth filled people's hearts with her gentle, giving nature.

For a while, she was well enough to send loving notes to Amy. But soon even those good spells were replaced by long periods of tossing and turning. Beth would speak incoherently or sink into a heavy sleep. The doctor started coming twice a day. Hannah stayed up most nights. Jo never left Beth's side. Meg readied a telegram, just in case.

December blew in carrying misery and fear. When the doctor came that morning, he told Hannah to send for Mrs. March.

Jo dashed to the post office. When she returned home, Laurie arrived with a letter from Mr. Brooke saying their father was once again on the mend. The boy immediately noticed Jo's long, sad face and asked, "What's wrong? Is Beth worse?"

Jo nodded. "I've sent for Mother."

"Was it your idea?"

"No. The doctor told us to."

Laurie looked startled. "It's not that bad, is it?"

"Yes," Jo said, sobbing. "She doesn't even know us anymore. She no longer looks like my Beth. With both Mother and Father gone, I just can't bear it." The tears streamed down her face.

Laurie took her hand and whispered, "I'm here. Hold on to me, Jo."

"Thank you Laurie. I'm better now."

He said quietly, "Keep hoping for the best. Your mother will be here soon."

A fresh rainfall of tears started. "Oh Laurie! Beth is my conscience and I *can't* give her up! I can't!"

Laurie choked back his tears and said, "I don't think she'll die. She's so good, and we all love her so much."

"The good and dear people always do die!" Jo groaned, but she stopped crying.

"You stay here," he said. "I'll make you feel better in a minute." When he returned, he was carrying a glass of wine.

Jo took it and proposed a toast, "To the health of my dear Beth!" She sipped slowly and said, "You're a good doctor, Laurie, and such a good friend. How can I ever repay you?"

"That's not necessary. Besides, I've got a surprise."

"What?"

He smiled. "I telegraphed your mother yesterday. Brooke replied that she'd come home at once. She'll be here tonight!"

Jo flew out of her chair and threw her arms around his neck. "Oh Laurie! I'm so glad." She laughed and trembled and held on tight to the bewildered boy. He patted her back and then gave her a shy kiss, which brought her to her senses.

"I'm sorry," she said, "I couldn't help flying at you. No more wine for me! It makes me reckless."

Laurie fixed his tie. "Not to worry. I didn't mind. I'm going to pick up your mother. Her train gets in at two in the morning."

Jo smiled. "Really, Laurie, how can I thank you?"

"You can fly at me again," he teased. "I rather liked it."

"No thank you. Go home and rest. It's going to be a long night. Bless you Laurie, bless you!"

For a moment, it was as if a burst of sunshine had entered the house. Everyone was so happy to hear that Marmee was finally coming home. Everyone but Beth, who lay in a heavy stupor. Meg and Jo hovered over her, because the doctor wasn't expected to return until midnight when some change might occur.

They all waited, but no one slept. It was past two when Meg came into the parlor with an ashen face. Jo had the dreadful thought, "Beth has died and she's afraid to tell me." She flew

upstairs to Beth's bedside. The flush of the fever and the look of pain were gone from her young face. She looked so peaceful. Jo leaned over her dear sister and said, "Good-bye, my Beth, good-bye."

Jo's tearful speech woke Hannah from her slumber. The servant hurried to the bed and felt Beth's forehead. She smiled broadly and said, "The fever's turned! She's sleeping normally. Thank goodness."

Soon the girls let Dr. Bangs in, who confirmed Hannah's diagnosis. Beth had pulled through! Meg and Jo hugged and kissed each other. With the good news and the jingling bells announcing the arrival of their mother's carriage, there were never two happier girls.

# CHAPTER 16

## Confidential

ﻌﺷ

Mrs. March did not leave Beth's side after returning home that morning. Meg and Jo were able to sleep peacefully now that their mother was home. The next day was bright and cheerful.

Laurie went to see Amy at Aunt March's. Amy had been wishing and wishing that her sister would get better. Even though she almost worried herself sick, she also did her best to be brave. Aunt March had been keeping her busy, but she was still very homesick, and longed to be back in the familiar warmth of her family.

Laurie smiled as told her the good news. She tried hard to conceal her longing to go home and see her mother. But Beth was still sick so she had to settle for writing a note.

Much to her surprise and delight, her mother arrived at Aunt March's just as she was putting pen to paper. Amy sat on Marmee's lap, relating her hardships. Her mother kissed her in return. That day, Aunt March had given Amy a turquoise ring. Amy asked her mother if she could keep it.

Marmee replied, "I think you might be too young."

"But I'd like to wear it, to remind me of something."

"Of Aunt March?"

Amy shook her head. "No, to remind me not to be selfish." She explained, "Being selfish is my worst fault. Beth isn't selfish and that's why everyone loves her. I want to be better, yet I often forget.

But I could if I had something to remind me."

Marmee said, "Well, do your best, dear. And wear your ring. Now, I must get back to Beth. You'll be home soon enough."

Later that evening back at home, Jo slipped upstairs to talk to her mother. The burden of Laurie's secret had become too heavy. She told her mother about Meg's lost glove. After she finished, her mother asked, "Do you think Meg cares for Mr. Brooke?"

Jo responded, "Christopher Columbus! I don't know anything about love. Meg doesn't act like the heroines in my books. She doesn't faint and she has all her wits."

"Then you think she's not interested in John?"

Jo cried, "Who?"

"Mr. Brooke. I call him John now, since he was so kind to us at the hospital."

"Oh no!" Jo groaned. "You'll let Meg marry him just because he's been kind to Father."

Marmee quietly explained that John Brooke was an honorable young man. He had already spoken to Mr. March about his feelings toward Meg. He had asked Meg's father's permission to work hard for her—to make something of himself. Although he was an excellent man, Meg's parents still couldn't agree to her becoming engaged while she was only seventeen.

Jo complained, "I wish I could marry her myself just to keep her in the family."

Marmee smiled. Then, she asked Jo not to mention anything to Meg. She first wanted to see how Meg felt about Mr. Brooke.

"Mercy me!" Jo cried. "My heart will break if he comes back with a fortune and Meg falls in love with him."

"Jo, dear," Marmee began, "I want all my girls to have homes of their own in time. But Meg is still very young, and it will be some time before John can make a home for her."

"Wouldn't it be better if Meg married a rich man?"

"Money is a useful part of life, but so are love and virtue. Being rich with love is always better than having a fortune."

Mrs. March encouraged Jo to leave these matters to time, which would settle all questions of love and marriage. Jo listened carefully, even though it made her terribly sad to think of losing her Meg.

The secret weighed heavily upon Jo the next day. Meg noticed the change in her sister, though she didn't say anything. She learned long ago that the best way to get Jo to talk was not to ask questions. Only this time Jo remained quiet, assuming a cold manner. This annoyed Meg, which made Jo even more disagreeable.

Meg took comfort in her mother and soon ignored poor Jo. Laurie became Jo's only escape. There was one problem. He knew she had a secret and constantly tried to find out what it was. Jo never told him, but Laurie figured it had to be about Meg and Mr. Brooke. Finally, he set up his own bit of mischief.

For a couple of days, Meg was out of sorts. Jo assumed the worst—that Meg had fallen in love with Mr. Brooke.

"What shall we do?" she groaned to her mother.

"Nothing," Mrs. March said. "We wait until your father comes home. He'll settle everything."

The next day, Jo distributed the letters from the post office. There was a sealed one for Meg, who, after opening it, let out a scream.

"What's the matter?" Marmee asked.

"It's all a mistake! He didn't send it!" Meg cried. "Jo, how could you do it?"

"Me?" Jo said, "I didn't do anything! What's she talking about, Marmee?"

Meg's eyes were angry as she pulled a crumpled note from her pocket. She threw it at Jo and said, "You and that Laurie wrote it. How could you be so mean?"

The note was a love letter, supposedly from Mr. Brooke.

Jo exclaimed, "Oh, that little villain. He's playing tricks because I wouldn't tell him the secret."

Marmee, who knew Jo loved pranks, asked sternly, "Did you really have nothing to do with this?"

"Absolutely not! I swear."

Mrs. March turned to Meg. "Did you respond?"

The elder daughter blushed a deep rose. "I did!"

Meg confessed the whole story. Laurie had given Meg the first letter. She had responded to it with a note to Mr. Brooke saying she was too young to marry. Then, she had received a letter from Mr. Brooke saying that he had never sent the first letter and that Jo had played a prank. Meg was mortified.

Jo examined both letters carefully. "Here's the trick," she exclaimed. "Laurie's written both letters—the rogue."

Mrs. March sent for Laurie. She was going to put an end to such silly behavior. With Jo gone, she told Meg about Mr. Brooke's feelings toward her. Then, she gently asked, "What are your own?"

Meg replied that she didn't really know. The whole situation with the letters had scared her so much that she might never want to love someone. She begged Marmee not to tell Mr. Brooke. Her pride was immensely wounded.

After Laurie and Marmee spent a long time in the study, Jo and Meg were called into the room.

Laurie looked so ashamed that Jo forgave him right then. He apologized honestly and profusely. He swore that he would never do anything like that again.

Everyone forgave Laurie and soon the prank was forgotten, except by lovely Meg. Her mind wandered often to thoughts of that certain someone. Once Jo even found a piece of paper on which Meg had written, "Mrs. John Brooke." Jo groaned tragically and threw the paper into the fire. Laurie's prank may very well have quickened the day Meg would leave.

# CHAPTER 17

# Pleasant Prospects

The weeks leading up to Christmas were peaceful. Mr. March sent word he'd be home early in the new year. Beth was improving every day. Amy was home from her aunt's. Everyone was busy preparing for a very merry holiday.

Christmas Day itself was crowned with good feeling. Beth was able to stand by the window and admire the brilliant snow maiden Jo and Laurie had built for her. Presents were distributed, and all were pleased with their gifts.

Beth said, "I'm so happy. If only Father

was here." The other girls heartily agreed.

The impish Laurie poked his head through the parlor door and called, "One more present for the March family!"

Suddenly, their beloved father appeared. In an instant, all pairs of loving arms embraced him. There were hugs, kisses, giggles, and even a few happy tears.

There was never such a Christmas dinner as they had that day. Hannah had cooked a big, juicy turkey. The dinner table was filled with all the trimmings. Mr. Laurence, Laurie, and Mr. Brooke joined the March family.

"It was just a year ago that we all complained about the miserable Christmas we expected," Jo pointed out.

"The year ended up being pleasant on the whole, didn't it?" Meg asked as she quietly thought about Mr. Brooke's handsome eyes.

Then Amy said, "It's been a very hard year, too."

"I'm so glad it's over," Beth commented, looking at her father, "because now we have you back."

Mr. March smiled at his brood of lovely daughters. He congratulated each for working hard and overcoming her faults, and for being kind and considerate. But most of all, he praised them for loving each other and truly becoming his "Little Women."

Before Beth played the piano, she recalled reading about a pleasant green meadow where lilies bloomed all year. This loving mood continued with the singing of hymns. The air was filled with happy voices and fond wishes for a Merry Christmas to all.

The next day, regular chores were neglected as mother and daughters tended to Mr. March.

Jo grumbled at the umbrella Mr. Brooke had left behind. Poor Meg was absentminded, shy, and silent, blushing whenever John's name was mentioned. The underlying question weighed heavily upon Mr. and Mrs. March.

Meg and Jo had a heart-to-heart talk after they watched Laurie stagger around outside the window, pretending to be a wounded lover.

"What would you say if he did ask?" Jo wondered.

"Well, I'd be calm. I'd say, 'Thank you, Mr. Brooke, you are very kind, but I'm too young to be engaged.' "

Jo laughed. "I don't think you'll say that!"

"Yes I will. Then, I'll walk out of the room with dignity."

Meg rose to show Jo exactly how she'd leave— only to bump into Mr. Brooke. Jo slipped out to give Meg the chance to make her speech.

"Good afternoon," Mr. Brooke said calmly. "I

came for my umbrella and to see how your
father's doing today."

Meg said, "It's very well, he's in the rack. I'll
get him and tell it you were here." In her nerv-
ousness, she had confused her father with the
umbrella!

"Are you afraid of me, Margaret?" Mr. Brooke
looked so hurt that Meg blushed.

"How can I be afraid of you?" she said. "You've
been so kind to my father. I wish I could thank
you."

"Should I tell you how?" He held tightly to
her small hand.

Meg desperately tried to withdraw her hand.
"Oh, please don't."

"I just want to know if you love me a little,
because I love you so very much."

This was the time for the calm, proper speech.
Only Meg forgot every word! Instead, she stut-
tered, "I'm far too young." Annoyed by his

assumption of success, Meg pulled her hand free and said, "Now please, go away!"

If a broken heart could be reflected in a face, then that's how poor Mr. Brooke looked. "Is that really what you want?"

"Yes. Father thinks I shouldn't worry about such things. And I don't intend to."

"Could you change your mind? I'll wait if you need more time."

Meg's eyes blazed and her tone changed. "I would rather you didn't think of me at all!"

He turned very pale. Meg felt her heart relenting, but Aunt March walked into the house at that moment. She saw the pair and asked angrily, "What's going on here?"

Mr. Brooke vanished into the other room and Meg replied, "Nothing. It's just a friend of Father's who has come to see how he's doing." She pulled herself together. "I'm surprised to see you, Aunt March."

"Obviously. You are beet red. I demand to know what's going on here."

"Mr. Brooke and I were just talking."

Aunt March grunted, "So that's Brooke, the tutor. You haven't accepted his proposal, have you?"

Meg was very upset now. "Shh. He'll hear you. Please, I'll get Mother."

"One minute, child," Aunt March insisted. "I have something I want to say." It was Meg's duty, she explained, to marry a rich man and save her family. She should not marry a poor man with no prospects.

The thought of someone thinking so little of "her" John angered Meg. She praised John as being kind and generous. "I'll marry whom I please," she said. "My John isn't a rich man, but I know I'll be happy because he loves me!"

After uttering harsh words, Aunt March turned and slammed the door in Meg's face. Meg didn't know whether to laugh or cry. John came back into the hallway, having overheard the conversation. He said quietly, "We'll be happy together, won't we, Meg?"

Meg looked up at his kind, handsome face and said, "Yes, John."

John spent the rest of the afternoon convincing Mr. and Mrs. March of his good intentions. The entire family soon accepted the engagement. Even Jo came around once she saw how happy her sister was with John.

They had a lovely dinner to celebrate the engagement. Laurie came over with a beautiful bouquet of flowers, and Mr. Laurence brought a bottle of champagne. As the sun fell, a happy group gathered in the parlor. The young couple was excited about their plans. A more pleasant picture could not be imagined. The reunited family sat happily around the fireplace with good friends and joyful thoughts for the future.

## What Do *You* Think?
### Questions for Discussion

∽

Have you ever been around a toddler who keeps asking the question "Why?" Does your teacher call on you in class with questions from your homework? Do your parents ask you questions at the dinner table about your day? We are always surrounded by questions that need a specific response. But is it possible to have a question with no right answer?

The following questions are about the book you just read. But this is not a quiz! They are designed to help you look at the people, places, and events in the story from different angles. These questions so not have specific answers. Instead, they might make you think of the story in a completely new way.

Think carefully about each question and enjoy discovering more about this classic story.

1. When Mrs. March returns on Christmas, she says to the girls, "A very poor family lives nearby. They have no fire and are very hungry. Will you girls give them your breakfast as a Christmas present?" How does this action reflect the true spirit of Christmas? What would you have done?

2. Jo has a special place in the attic where she loves to eat apples and read. Why is it important for Jo to have a place of her own? If you had your own special room in the attic, what would it look like?

3. Meg and Jo develop a signal system in case Jo acts improperly at the dance. Have you ever

had a secret code in case you or a friend needed help? What was it?

4. The author says of the March sisters, "All in all, they were happy girls who found comfort in one another, when the outside world was so disappointing." Do you feel that way about your brothers and sisters? If you are an only child, do you have this kind of relationship with any of your friends?

5. Mrs. March tells the girls, "When you feel unhappy, count your blessings and be grateful— for there are always those in the world with less." Do you agree? What blessings are you grateful for?

6. In chapter 6, "Amy's Valley of Humiliation," the author says that Amy always used wrong words. Have you ever used a word in the wrong way or heard someone else do so? Did you correct that person?

7. Do you think Amy acted properly in punishing Jo for not taking her to the show? How would you have reacted?

8. How does Jo's temper get her into trouble? Does Jo really have a bad temper or is she just impulsive?

9. Jo sells her hair to help pay for her mother's trip to Washington. What is the biggest sacrifice you have ever made for your family?

10. Jo is very concerned that Meg will grow up and get married. Why do you think she is so worried?

# Afterword

*by Arthur Pober, EdD*

 споро

First impressions are important.

Whether we are meeting new people, going to new places, or picking up a book unknown to us, first impressions count for a lot. They can lead to warm, lasting memories or can make us shy away from any future encounters.

Can you recall your own first impressions and earliest memories of reading the classics?

Do you remember wading through pages and pages of text to prepare for an exam? Or were you the child who hid under the blanket to read with a flashlight, joining forces with Robin Hood to save Maid Marian? Do you remember only how long it took you to read a lengthy novel such as *Little Women*? Or did you become best friends with the March sisters?

Even for a gifted young reader, getting through long chapters with dense language can easily become overwhelming and can obscure the richness of the story and its characters. Reading an abridged, newly crafted version of a classic novel can be the gentle introduction a child needs to explore the characters and story line without the frustration of difficult vocabulary and complex themes.

Reading an abridged version of a classic novel gives the young reader a sense of independence and the satisfaction of finishing a "grown-up" book. And when a child is engaged with and inspired by a classic story, the tone is set for further exploration of the story's themes, characters, history, and details. As a child's reading skills advance, the desire to tackle the original, unabridged version of the story will naturally emerge.

If made accessible to young readers, these stories can become invaluable tools for understanding themselves in the context of their families and social environments. This is why the Classic Starts series includes questions that stimulate discussion regarding the impact and social relevance of the characters and stories today. These questions can foster lively conversations between children and their parents or teachers. When we look at the issues, values, and standards of past times in terms of how we live now, we can appreciate literature's classic tales in a very personal and engaging way.

Share your love of reading the classics with a young child, and introduce an imaginary world real enough to last a lifetime.

# Dr. Arthur Pober, EdD

Dr. Arthur Pober has spent more than twenty years in the fields of early-childhood and gifted education. He is the former principal of one of the world's oldest laboratory schools for gifted youngsters, Hunter College Elementary School, and former director of Magnet Schools for the Gifted and Talented for more than 25,000 youngsters in New York City.

Dr. Pober is a recognized authority in the areas of media and child protection and is currently the U.S. representative to the European Institute for the Media and European Advertising Standards Alliance.

Explore these wonderful stories in our
Classic Starts™ library.